This book belongs to:

Contents

Cover illustration by Valeria Petrone

Published by Ladybird Books Ltd
27 Wrights Lane London W8 5TZ
A Penguin Company

2 4 6 8 10 9 7 5 3 1

© LADYBIRD BOOKS LTD MCMXCVII, MMI

LADYBIRD and the device of a Ladybird are trademarks of Ladybird Books Ltd

Printed in Italy

My mum is mad

written by Lorraine Horsley
illustrated by Valeria Petrone

My sister is bossy.

My dog is bad.

My brother is noisy.

My mum is mad.

My granny is wacky.

My grandad is late.

My dad's pushed
the button...

My family is great!

The new babies

written by Shirley Jackson

illustrated by Ann Kronheimer

I went to the house next
door with Dad.

We went to see
the new babies.

I looked in the basket.
I saw two little black noses…

and two little white faces.

I saw two puppies.

Dad said, "Choose one!"

But which one?

I wanted to be

written by Shirley Jackson
illustrated by Julie Anderson

I wanted to be an
astronaut.

But Mum said, "No!"

I wanted to be a painter,
but Mum said, "No!"

I wanted to be a doctor,
but Mum said, "No!"

I wanted to be a diver,
but Mum said, "No!"

I wanted to be a gardener,
but Mum said, "No!"

I wanted to be a writer,
and Mum said, "Yes!"

Bouncing basketball

written by Shirley Jackson
illustrated by Jan Smith

I had a bouncing basketball.
I bounced it up and down.

I bounced it through
the house

and I bounced it
through the town.

I bounced the ball quite slowly.

I bounced the ball quite fast.

I bounced it through
the town again...

and bounced
back home
at last!

I wanted to be

Read the first two pages of the story
to your child as this will introduce it. Help him to read
the rest to you. Talk about the different occupations
explored by the child. What would your child like to be
when he grows up?

Bouncing basketball

Read this rhyme to your child and encourage him
to read it with you, like a song, before he reads it on
his own. Try singing it to the tune of 'I had a little
nut tree…' Help him to notice the spelling patterns
in the rhyming words:

d͜own   t͜own   f͜ast   l͜ast

Point out the **-ed** ending in 'bounced'.

New words

Encourage your child to use these
new words to make up and write
his own stories and rhymes.

Go back to look at the stories and wordlists
in Books 1 – 8 to practise the other words used.

Read with Ladybird

Read with Ladybird has been written to help you to help your child:

- to take the first steps in reading
- to improve early reading progress
- to gain confidence

Main Features

- **Several stories and rhymes in each book**

This means that there is not too much for you and your child to read in one go.

- **Rhyme and rhythm**

Read with Ladybird uses rhymes or stories with a rhythm to help your child to predict and memorise new words.

- **Gradual introduction and repetition of key words**

Read with Ladybird introduces and repeats the 100 most frequently used words in the English language.

- **Compatible with school reading schemes**

The key words that your child will learn are compatible with the word lists that are used in schools. This means that you can be confident that practising at home will support work done at school.

- **Information pullout**

Use this pullout to understand more about how you can use each story to help your child to learn to read.

But the most important feature of **Read with Ladybird** is for you and your child to have fun sharing the stories and rhymes with each other.